Dedication

I dedicate this book to Becca Cooper.
May God's light shine upon you and
continue to guide you. Your love for others
will bring people closer to the heart of
God. May He shower you with blessings,
protection and grace.

Maria A Flores

This Book Belongs To:

The Bible is Your Compass

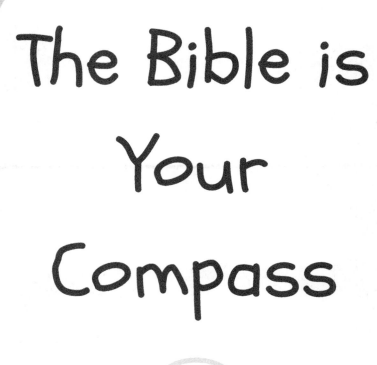

SAFARI
COLORING & ACTIVITY
BOOK

Biblical Affirmations for Children

By: Maria A Flores

Touch the Heart, Reach the Soul LLC
Polk City, FL, USA

Safari Coloring & Activity Book: Biblical Affirmations for Children

2024 Copyright by Touch the Heart, Reach the Soul LLC

BOOKS, APPAREL, HOME DECOR, JEWELRY,
ORIGINAL ART & GIFT ITEMS:
http://touchtheheartreachthesoul.store
customerservice@touchtheheartreachthesoul.com

REFERENCES:
The Holy Bible, English Standard Version. (1983). Good News Publishers.
Search for your favorite animals! (n.d.) https://a-z-animals.com

Manuscript, design, illustrations, and book cover by Maria A Flores

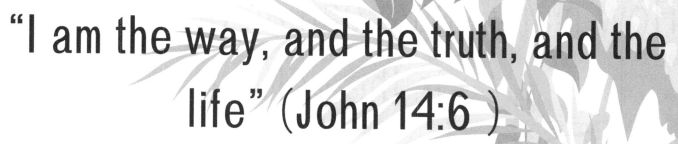

"I am the way, and the truth, and the life" (John 14:6)

How many years can an elephant live in the wild?

Which elephants have the longest ears: African or Asian?

"As the Father has loved me, so I have loved you. Abide in my love" (John 15:9)

What country has the largest number of wild tigers?

On average, how many meals a week do tigers eat?

"For God so loved the world, that He gave His only Son..." (John 3:16)

What do zebras weigh? (HINT: heavy!)

What do zebras like to eat?

"But those that were sown on good soil... bear fruit" (Mark 4:20)

Which are larger: apes or gorillas?

Gorillas inhabit the tropical forests of _____.

"Even though I walk through the valley of the shadow of death, I will fear no evil" (Psalms 23:4)

How fast can lions run?

Where do lions like to live?

"Take no part in the unfruitful works of darkness, but instead expose them" (Ephesians 5:11)

How much does the smallest monkey in the world weigh?

Is it legal to own a monkey as a pet in the USA?

"No city or house divided against itself will stand" (Matthew 12:25)

How many types of snake species exist worldwide?

Do snakes chew their food?

"I tell you, do not be anxious about your life; instead seek his kingdom and these things will be added to you" (Luke 12: 22, 31)

Wild boars are known for their sharp ____.

Are wild boars known for attacking humans?

"The thief comes only to steal, kill, and destroy. I came that they may have life and have it abundantly" (John 10: 10)

What do crocodiles like to eat?

Can crocodiles be dangerous to humans?

"You are my beloved Son; with you I am well pleased" (Mark 1: 11)

How long is the tongue of a giraffe?

What is the average weight of a giraffe?

"I have baptized you with water, but He will baptize you with the Holy Spirit" (Mark 1: 8)

Kangaroos can hop _feet in a single motion.

There are many kangaroos in this country: __.

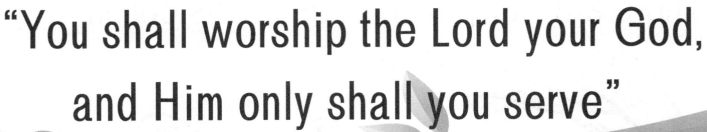

"You shall worship the Lord your God, and Him only shall you serve" (Luke 4: 8)

Hippopotamuses can weigh between

___-___ pounds.

Hippos are known for being _____.

"... But he grew strong in his faith as he gave glory to God" (Romans 4: 20)

A tortoise can live up to ___ years.

Do tortoises like to live on the sand or in the water?

"For nothing will be impossible with God" (Luke 1: 37)

How long does it take before the feathers of a flamingo turn pink?

Why do flamingos stand on one leg?

"A faithful man will abound with blessings..." (Proverbs 28: 20)

Are tarantulas poisonous?

Where do tarantulas like to live?

Answers to Trivia questions

Elephants: African elephants, 70 years

Tigers: India, one meal per week

Zebras: weight 386-992 lbs; eat plants, also shrubs, bark

Gorillas: Gorillas are larger than other ape species, Africa

Lions: 35 mph, open woodland; variety of prey available

Monkeys: weighs less 1 lb!, illegal in most states

Snakes: 4000 species; they swallow their food

Wild Boars: Teeth! Yes, they attack humans

Crocodiles: birds, fish, frogs, bugs; Yes. beware!

Giraffes: 18 inches! 13- 20 feet

Kangaroos: 30 feet in single hop! Australia

Hippopotamuses: 2,200-9,900 lbs, aggressive

Tortoises: 150 years! Sandy soil, close to water

Flamingos: 2-3 years, use less energy & stay warm

Tarantulas: YES; under rocks, logs, trees

SAFARI

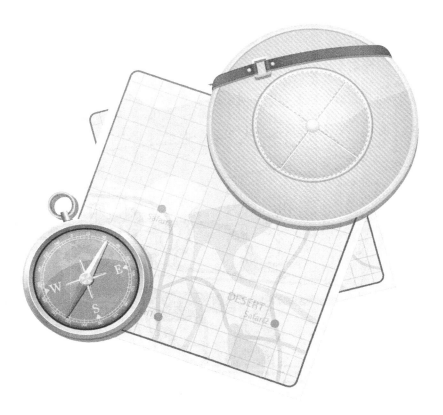

Affirmations for Children

Life is a journey, full of surprises.

As you embark on your journey, keep God at the center.

I select my friends wisely.

I am a child of God.

I can do all things through Christ.

I am loved.

I am worthy of love.

I have purpose in my life.

Holy Spirit, guide me.

I will call on Jesus when I need help.

Angels smiled when I was born.

I belong to a family.

I am never alone.

I have a Heavenly Father.

I have a bright future.

I am safe and secure.

God knew me before I was born.

The Lord has a plan for me.

I am blessed and protected by God.

I will keep my heart humble.

God speaks to me and I listen.

I have complete peace in my life.

I can make good decisions.

I find ways to bless the people around me.

I was created in God's image.

I have perfect peace in Christ.

My mission has just begun.

I am wanted and loved.

I am special and unique.

I will follow the straight and narrow path.

My guardian angel watches over me.

The Lord has a plan for me.

I am strong and courageous.

I am smart and creative.

I walk in wisdom.

I talk to my Heavenly Father.

I can see the good in people.

I am slow to anger.

I sleep well and feel rested.

I will trust in you, Lord.

I allow the Holy Spirit to help me.

Draw a picture of YOU!

Draw your favorite animal that lives in a jungle.

If you have enjoyed this book, please write a review on Amazon.

To see the full collection of books from TOUCH THE HEART, REACH THE SOUL visit us at http://touchtheheartreachthesoul.store

Made in the USA
Middletown, DE
03 September 2024

60016952R00071